# Litter B



"You guys sure are good at picking up garbage," Bruce Patman said in a taunting voice. He took a big gulp from the can of soda he was holding. "But you're wasting your time."

"Oh, really?" Elizabeth said, feeling angry. She and Jessica and their classmates were all helping to turn a garbage-filled city lot into a park.

"My dad is just going along with this for fun," Bruce boasted. "He's definitely going to buy this piece of land and build a garage. It'll make him a lot of money."

Jessica pointed her finger at him. "He doesn't get to decide. The city council does."

Bruce just smiled. Then he took the last swallow of soda and dropped the can on the ground. "Here's some more litter for you to pick up." He laughed and walked away.

Bantam Skylark Books in the
SWEET VALLEY KIDS series

#1 SURPRISE! SURPRISE!
#2 RUNAWAY HAMSTER
#3 THE TWINS' MYSTERY TEACHER
#4 ELIZABETH'S VALENTINE
#5 JESSICA'S CAT TRICK
#6 LILA'S SECRET
#7 JESSICA'S BIG MISTAKE
#8 JESSICA'S ZOO ADVENTURE
#9 ELIZABETH'S SUPER-SELLING LEMONADE
#10 THE TWINS AND THE WILD WEST
#11 CRYBABY LOIS
#12 SWEET VALLEY TRICK OR TREAT
#13 STARRING WINSTON EGBERT
#14 JESSICA THE BABY-SITTER
#15 FEARLESS ELIZABETH
#16 JESSICA THE TV STAR
#17 CAROLINE'S MYSTERY DOLLS
#18 BOSSY STEVEN
#19 JESSICA AND THE JUMBO FISH
#20 THE TWINS GO TO THE HOSPITAL
#21 JESSICA AND THE SPELLING BEE SURPRISE
#22 SWEET VALLEY SLUMBER PARTY
#23 LILA'S HAUNTED HOUSE PARTY
#24 COUSIN KELLY'S FAMILY SECRET
#25 LEFT-OUT ELIZABETH
#26 JESSICA'S SNOBBY CLUB
#27 THE SWEET VALLEY CLEANUP TEAM
#28 ELIZABETH MEETS HER HERO
#29 ANDY AND THE ALIEN

SWEET VALLEY KIDS SUPER SNOOPER EDITIONS
#1 THE CASE OF THE SECRET SANTA
#2 THE CASE OF THE MAGIC CHRISTMAS BELL
#3 THE CASE OF THE HAUNTED CAMP

SWEET VALLEY KIDS

# THE SWEET VALLEY CLEANUP TEAM

Written by
Molly Mia Stewart

Created by
FRANCINE PASCAL

Illustrated by
Ying-Hwa Hu

A BANTAM SKYLARK BOOK®
NEW YORK • TORONTO • LONDON • SYDNEY • AUCKLAND

RL 2, 005–008

THE SWEET VALLEY CLEANUP TEAM
*A Bantam Skylark Book / March 1992*

*Sweet Valley High® and Sweet Valley Kids are trademarks of Francine Pascal*

*Conceived by Francine Pascal*

*Produced by Daniel Weiss Associates, Inc.*
*33 West 17th Street*
*New York, NY 10011*

*Cover art by Susan Tang*

*Skylark Books is a registered trademark of Bantam Books, a division of Bantam Doubleday Dell Publishing Group, Inc. Registered in U.S. Patent and Trademark Office and elsewhere.*



ISBN 0-553-15923-2

*Published simultaneously in the United States and Canada*

---

*Bantam Books are published by Bantam Books, a division of Bantam Doubleday Dell Publishing Group, Inc. Its trademark, consisting of the words "Bantam Books" and the portrayal of a rooster, is Registered in U.S. Patent and Trademark Office and in other countries. Marca Registrada. Bantam Books, 666 Fifth Avenue, New York, New York 10103.*

---

PRINTED IN THE UNITED STATES OF AMERICA

OPM 0 9 8 7 6 5 4 3 2

*To Michael Bloom*

## CHAPTER 1

# Keep Sweet Valley Sweet

"Look," Elizabeth Wakefield said as she poured herself some orange juice. "Our avocado pit is starting to grow."

Her twin sister, Jessica, got up from the breakfast table to look at the large pit that was in a jar on the windowsill. It had cracked down the middle and a green shoot was sprouting from the crack. "How long will it take to grow into a tree?"

"I don't know," Mrs. Wakefield said. "They grow pretty fast. Almost as fast as you two."

Elizabeth and Jessica were in second grade at Sweet Valley Elementary School. Both of them had blond hair and blue-green eyes. They looked almost exactly alike. In fact, even their close friends sometimes had to check the twins' name bracelets to tell them apart.

On the inside, though, Elizabeth and Jessica were as different as could be. Elizabeth studied hard in school and was proud of the good grades she got. Jessica liked school, too, but only because it gave her a chance to talk to her friends.

Despite their differences, Elizabeth and Jessica shared everything, from secrets to sandwiches. Being different didn't keep them from being best friends.

"I love plants," Elizabeth said, going over for a closer look at the avocado pit. "Green is my favorite color. And flowers smell so sweet."

Mr. Wakefield walked into the kitchen just in time to hear Elizabeth's last comment. "That reminds me of something I read in the newspaper yesterday," he said. "Have you kids heard of a group called Keep Sweet Valley Sweet?"

"What do they do?" the twins' older brother, Steven, asked through a mouthful of cereal. "Sprinkle sugar on everything?"

Mr. Wakefield laughed. "Not quite. They try to make sure that there are plenty of nice trees and flowers and parks in the city," he explained.

"That's a good idea," Jessica said. "I love playing at the park after school."

Mr. Wakefield went over to the counter and poured himself a cup of coffee. He always drank a cup before leaving for the law firm where he worked. "The article said that this group is trying to turn an empty lot downtown into a park. The problem is that it's also the perfect spot to put a parking garage for the new mini-mall."

"Who needs another parking garage?" Elizabeth asked. "There are too many of them already. I'd rather have a park."

SWEET VALLEY NEWS

"Not everyone feels that way," Mr. Wakefield said. "A very rich man named Mr. Patman wants to buy that property and build the garage. The city council owns the land, and they're thinking of selling to him."

"That's not fair," Jessica said. "I bet everyone else in town would vote for a park."

"It sounds as if you agree with Keep Sweet Valley Sweet, Jessica," Mrs. Wakefield said.

"I do, too," Elizabeth said. "Mr. Patman must be a mean man."

"There's a rich kid in third grade named Bruce Patman," Steven said. "He's a stuck-up spoiled brat. I bet that's his father."

Jessica and Elizabeth looked at each other. They both knew who Bruce Patman was, even though they had never spoken to him. He often got picked up at the park in a big, fancy limousine.

"Who makes the final decision about the lot?" Mrs. Wakefield asked her husband.

Mr. Wakefield took another sip of coffee. "The city council does. They're in favor of building the garage, and they could really use the money from the sale of the land. Many people do want a park, though, so the council is giving Keep Sweet Valley Sweet some time to try to prove that a park would benefit the town more than a garage would."

"How?" Jessica wanted to know. It all sounded very complicated to her. She couldn't understand why anyone would rather have a parking garage than a park.

"By cleaning up the junk, putting in some plants, things like that," Mr. Wakefield replied. "Unfortunately, they're going to have a tough time getting the place fixed up. They don't have enough workers. It's just a volunteer group."

Elizabeth frowned and poured some milk onto her cereal. She didn't think it was fair that Mr. Patman should automatically get his way because he was rich. And it wouldn't be fair if Keep Sweet Valley Sweet lost just because they didn't have enough people to help them.

Suddenly she had an idea. "Maybe we could pitch in! It could be a class project," she suggested, sounding excited.

"Good idea," agreed Jessica. "If we turn it into a park everyone will see that it's better than an ugly parking garage."

Mr. Wakefield smiled. "Elizabeth, you're brilliant! That sounds like a perfect plan."

## CHAPTER 2

# Ecology

At the beginning of science class that day, the twins' teacher, Mrs. Otis, made an announcement. "We're beginning our unit on ecology," she said. "Who can tell me what ecology is?"

Todd Wilkins raised his hand. "It's cleaning up pollution, and recycling, and things like that."

"And Earth Day," Eva Simpson said. "That's the day when everyone is especially careful not to hurt the environment."

Mrs. Otis smiled. "That's right. Earth Day is a good time to learn what we should be doing to help the environment all year round."

The teacher put a large, bulging paper bag on her desk. "I'm glad Todd mentioned recycling," she said, "because for our first ecology project we're going to do a little recycling ourselves."

While their teacher began to explain how to make recycled paper, Jessica leaned over toward Elizabeth's desk.

"Are we going to ask her?" she whispered.

Elizabeth nodded. "Let's do it as soon as she's finished talking."

A few minutes later, the class separated into smaller groups and began tearing newspapers, paper bags, and notebook paper into small scraps. Elizabeth and Jessica walked up to Mrs. Otis's desk.

"Yes, girls?" the teacher asked with a smile.

"We have an idea for a class project," Elizabeth said. "We want to prove that a park is better than a parking garage."

Jessica and Elizabeth took turns explaining everything their father had told them.

While they talked, Mrs. Otis nodded her head and looked very interested.

"I think that's a wonderful idea," she said when they were finished. "I'll get in touch with Keep Sweet Valley Sweet during recess and offer our help. Your idea fits in perfectly with our ecology unit. By helping to create a park in Sweet Valley, we'll be doing our part to make the world a greener, cleaner place."

"Great!" Jessica yelled, jumping up with one hand in the air. "We're going to save the planet!"

By recess, everyone in class had heard about the plan. Jessica was surrounded by kids asking questions. She loved being the center of attention, even though she didn't know the answers to all of the questions.

"How big would the parking garage be?" Amy Sutton asked.

Jessica made a face. "Probably at least *ten* stories high. All black."

"Are they going to start building it right away?" Winston Egbert wanted to know.

"Unless we stop them," Jessica said seriously.

Lila Fowler, who was Jessica's second best friend after Elizabeth, pointed across the playground. "There's Bruce Patman. His father's the one who wants to build the garage."

Immediately, everyone crowded around Lila instead of Jessica. "Do you think he knows about it?" Amy asked.

"Maybe. I'll go ask him," Lila said. She began walking across the playground.

"I'll go with you," Jessica said quickly.

Bruce Patman was playing kickball with a group of other third-grade boys. Lila marched right up to him, interrupting the game. "Is your father really buying the empty lot downtown and building a giant parking garage on it?" she asked him.

Bruce shrugged. "If he wants to, he will," he said in a snobby tone.

"We're going to stop him," Jessica said.

"Oh, I'm sure he's really worried," Bruce said, laughing.

Jessica frowned at him. "If we can clean up the lot and make a nice park there, the people in charge will tell him he can't build his ugly old garage."

"Sure they will," Bruce said, shaking his head. He took a pair of sunglasses out of his shirt pocket and put them on. "You might as well give up now. My father gets what he wants."

"Come on, Jessica," Lila said, putting her nose in the air. "Let's get out of here. It smells."

Jessica followed her friend. "He makes me so mad!" she said, clenching her fists.

"Me, too," said Lila. "He thinks he's so cool. I just hope we can save the park as a class project. Bruce thinks that just because his father is rich, he can do anything."

Jessica smiled. Lila's father was also very wealthy, and Lila sometimes thought that gave her the right to boss people around. But Jessica was glad Lila was on her side this time.

When recess was over, Jessica was the first one to return to the classroom. She could hardly wait to hear whether Mrs. Otis had talked to the Keep Sweet Valley Sweet people. Mrs. Otis didn't keep her waiting for long.

"We start on Saturday morning," the teacher announced. "We're going to make that city lot the prettiest park in Sweet Valley!"

# CHAPTER 3

# Cleaning Up

"This is going to be fun," Elizabeth said, looking out the window of the car. It was Saturday, and the twins were on their way to the empty lot.

"I hope we don't have to touch a lot of dirty stuff," Jessica said as Mrs. Wakefield stopped the car in front of a large, junk-filled lot. There was litter everywhere.

"You can have a long bubble bath when you get home," Mrs. Wakefield said. "So work hard, do what Mrs. Otis says, and no clowning around, OK? Eva's mother will drive you home."

"Yes, Mom," Elizabeth and Jessica said at the same time.

The twins jumped out of the car and ran over to the lot. Many of their classmates had already arrived, along with Mrs. Otis. Several other adults were there, too. Elizabeth guessed that they were the people from Keep Sweet Valley Sweet.

"What can we do to help?" Elizabeth asked a friendly-looking man who was standing with Mrs. Otis.

"The first thing we need to do is clear out all this junk," he replied, handing Elizabeth a trash bag. "My name is Mike. If you have any questions, just holler."

Elizabeth liked the way Mike smiled when he said "holler." She took the trash bag from him and looked around. She saw that Todd, Amy, Eva, Ken Matthews, and Winston Egbert were already hard at work. Todd and Eva were putting an empty crate into a wheelbarrow, Amy was raking leaves, and Ken and Winston were putting broken bricks into a pile.

"Let's pick up some garbage," Elizabeth

said to her sister. She bent down to pick up an old, twisted soda straw.

"There's a bottle top," Jessica said, pointing at the ground.

Elizabeth laughed. "Pick it up. It won't bite you."

Jessica wrinkled her nose. She bent over and very carefully and delicately picked up the bottle top. "Gross," she said grumpily as she tossed it into the trash bag Elizabeth was holding. "Maybe this wasn't such a good idea after all."

At that moment, Elizabeth saw something that she knew would make Jessica a lot happier about picking up trash. "Look," she said, pointing. "There's a van from the TV news."

"Where?" Jessica spun around, her eyes wide. "We're going to be on TV!" She grabbed the plastic bag from Elizabeth's hand and began stuffing it with trash from the ground as fast as she could pick it up.

Elizabeth walked back to ask Mike what else she could do. "Why don't you take these full garbage bags to my pickup truck," Mike said. "It's that red one over there. Just toss the bags in the back, if they're not too heavy."

More and more students and adult volunteers were arriving all the time. The television camera crews filmed everything for the evening news. Somehow Jessica always seemed to be working right where the camera was pointing. She pushed the wheelbarrow, sorted clear glass bottles from brown ones, and helped roll an old metal oil drum out of the way.

"I can't believe how many people came to help," Elizabeth said to Amy. They were standing in the shade for a moment to catch their breath. "I bet we'll be finished in one day."

"I hope so," Amy said. "Then we could fix up another empty lot next weekend, and another one and another one and—"

Suddenly Amy stopped speaking and stared over Elizabeth's shoulder. Elizabeth turned around to see what her friend was looking at. A long, black limousine had just stopped by the curb. The back door opened, and a tall, dark-haired man in a business suit got out. A moment later, Bruce Patman got out of the car, too.

"Look, it's Bruce. And that must be Mr. Patman," Elizabeth whispered.

Jessica came over to stand in the shade with her sister and Amy. All three of them watched as Mr. Patman strolled over to Mike and the other volunteers. He had a very confident attitude. While his father talked to the adults, Bruce walked around the lot. He stopped in front of the twins.

"You guys sure are good at picking up garbage," Bruce said in a taunting voice. He took a big gulp from the can of soda he was holding. "I hate to tell you, but you're wasting your time."

"Oh, really?" Elizabeth said, feeling angry.

"My dad is just going along with this for fun," Bruce boasted. "He's definitely going to

buy this piece of land and build the garage. It'll make him a ton of money."

Jessica glared at him. "He doesn't get to decide. The city council does. That's what my father said. And he's a lawyer, so he should know!"

Bruce just smiled. Then he took a last swallow of soda and dropped the can on the ground. "Here's some more litter for you to pick up." He laughed and walked back to the car.

Elizabeth shook her head and stared after him angrily. "He's an idiot." Jessica and Amy nodded in agreement.

CHAPTER 4

# Operation Community Garden

At noon, all of the volunteers stopped for a lunch break. Jessica and Elizabeth ate their bag lunches with Lila, Amy, Eva, and Ellen Riteman.

Jessica read the bottom of her lunch bag while she munched on an apple. "This bag is made from recycled paper," she said.

"Just like our science project," Elizabeth said.

"Attention, everyone," Mike said loudly. He stood up and waved his hands. "First of all, I want to thank everyone for a stupendous cleanup job. Look at this place. It's spotless!"

A loud cheer went up. Jessica looked around. That morning, the lot had been a dirty, smelly, gloomy place filled with trash. Now, even though it was still empty and bare, it looked much better. The dirt had been raked clean, scrap lumber was piled neatly, waiting to be recycled, and bags of trash were lined on the sidewalk, ready to be loaded onto Mike's truck.

"I wish everyone here would help me clean my half of our bedroom," Jessica whispered to Elizabeth. "It would be perfect in ten seconds flat."

"Phase Two of Operation Community Garden is about to begin," Mike went on. "Several garden centers and nurseries are bringing donations of plants, trees, and shrubs. They should be arriving any minute. So everyone grab a shovel and get ready to dig."

"I hope I get to plant some flowers," Jessica said.

"The TV cameras aren't here anymore," Todd teased. "Are you still going to dig in the dirt?"

Jessica dusted off her hands. "I'm so dirty already I don't care anymore," she said. "Besides, since I helped pick up all that yucky junk, I want to help with the fun stuff, too."

Soon several trucks arrived, filled with plants for the garden. The volunteers helped the drivers unload bushes, pots of flowers, and bags of wood chips and peat moss from the backs of the trucks. There were even some large rolls of grass turf which could be unrolled like carpets to create a lawn.

"OK, now I need some good artists," Mike said, picking up some buckets of paint and three brushes. "Any volunteers?"

Jessica, Lila, and Ellen all put their hands up at the same time. "What do we need to paint?" Ellen asked.

"Right this way." Mike led them to the large, empty oil drum. "If we get this looking nice, it will make the perfect garbage can."

"Can we paint flowers on it?" Jessica asked.

"And words?" Lila went on. "Like 'please don't litter'?"

Mike smiled and nodded. "It's up to you. Use your imagination."

The three girls eagerly grabbed brushes and got to work.

In another part of the new garden, Elizabeth was helping an adult volunteer named Maria to make a bench out of pieces of scrap lumber. They planned to make several benches so that visitors to the park would have a place to sit down and rest.

Everywhere Jessica looked, people were busy turning the empty lot into a beautiful garden. Ken and Amy were making paths with wood chips. Eva, Winston, and several other kids were helping Mike plant patches of pretty flowers in the new green grass. Todd

WOODCHIP

was turning an old sink into a birdbath, and Mrs. Otis was watering a newly planted tree with a hose.

"I can't believe this was just a junky old garbage heap this morning," Jessica said as she and Lila and Ellen took the paint back to Mike. "Now it's a real park."

"Nobody would want this to be turned into a parking garage now," Ellen said.

"That's right," Jessica said. "We really showed Mr. Patman."

"And Bruce," Lila added.

"I hope you kids are right," Mike said. He held out his hand for each of them to shake. "I want to thank you for helping out. We couldn't have done it without you."

Jessica felt ten feet tall. She was tired and dirty, but she had never felt so proud. She was positive that the city council would decide to keep the new community garden exactly the way it was.

But just in case, she crossed her fingers behind her back.

## CHAPTER 5

# Bad News

Elizabeth dreamed all night about picking up trash, planting flowers, and watering trees. When she opened her eyes in the morning, she almost expected to see leafy branches over her head.

"I wish we could go back to the garden today," she said to Jessica as they went downstairs for breakfast. "Just to see if it still looks as pretty."

"Maybe Mom and Dad will take us over there," Jessica said with a sleepy yawn. "Let's ask them."

Mr. and Mrs. Wakefield agreed to take a drive by the garden. "I want to see if it's really as beautiful as you two keep bragging," Mrs. Wakefield teased.

"It definitely is," Elizabeth said firmly.

Steven decided to come along, too, and after breakfast, they all got into the car and drove into downtown Sweet Valley.

"I painted flowers on an old garbage can," Jessica said. "Wait until you see it. It's beautiful."

"You told us five million times already," Steven said.

"The girls are proud of all their hard work," Mr. Wakefield pointed out. "Turning a junkyard into a park isn't something you do every day."

Elizabeth couldn't wait to see their garden again. When they turned onto Maple Street, she rolled down the window. "We're almost there!"

As soon as the car stopped, Elizabeth and Jessica jumped out and ran to the entrance of the garden. All of the plants sparkled with dew in the morning sunlight. The colorful trash can and handmade benches stood alongside the inviting wood-chip paths. Several birds were playing in the birdbath Todd had made.

"This is gorgeous!" Mrs. Wakefield said as she got out of the car and joined the twins in the garden. "I can't believe this is the same place where I dropped you off yesterday morning."

Jessica ran to the garbage can. It was painted with flowers and wide stripes of green, white, pink, blue, and yellow. "Keep Sweet Valley Sweet! Put Litter Here Please!" it read in bright orange letters.

"Isn't it nice?" Jessica asked with a proud smile.

"It certainly is. The whole garden is lovely," Mr. Wakefield said. "Let's sit on this bench for a minute and just enjoy it."

Elizabeth leaned over to smell a flower. When she looked up, she saw a woman walking toward them. The woman was carrying a notebook and a pen.

"Good morning!" the woman called out. "I'm from the *Sweet Valley News*. Do you mind if I ask you a few questions about the garden for the paper?"

Mr. and Mrs. Wakefield smiled. "Our girls were part of the team that worked here yesterday," Mrs. Wakefield said. "They're the ones you should talk to."

"My name is Beth Weatherby," the reporter said, shaking hands with each of the twins. "Did you know that the city council might still decide to put a parking garage here?"

Elizabeth felt her stomach do a somersault. "What do you mean?" she asked nervously.

"Well," said Ms. Weatherby. "The town council held a meeting last night. They feel that because of the new mini-mall down the block, this area really needs more parking space."

"That's so unfair," Mrs. Wakefield inter-

rupted angrily. "The kids put in so much hard work."

"I know," the reporter agreed. "But there's a lot of money to be made from a parking garage."

Jessica crossed her arms. "Who cares about money?"

"I bet it's Mr. Patman," Elizabeth said. "If he builds the garage, he gets to charge people money to park in it."

Ms. Weatherby nodded. "I'm afraid that's right."

"Well, that's not fair," Jessica said. "Mr. Patman is a big meanie."

The reporter wrote down what Jessica had said. "I'll use your comments. Thanks a lot for your time."

Some other people had come into the garden, and Ms. Weatherby went to interview them. Elizabeth and Jessica sat down on the bench next to their parents and Steven.

"It's so unfair," Elizabeth said. "There must be a way to change Mr. Patman's mind."

"I bet Bruce could talk him out of building that stupid garage if he wanted to," Jessica said grumpily. "But he's just as bad as his father. All he cares about is money."

"Girls, I want to tell you something," their father said in a serious voice. "First of all, we're very proud of what you did. You saw a problem, and you offered to help solve it."

"Nobody can take that accomplishment away from you," Mrs. Wakefield added.

Mr. Wakefield put his arms around Elizabeth's and Jessica's shoulders. "But I have to warn you. People sometimes make decisions that seem wrong to us. Even with all your hard work, this space might still end up as a garage."

Elizabeth looked at the trees and grass and flowers. She tried to picture a parking garage instead, but it only made her feel sad.

"We have to save our park," Jessica said firmly. "There has to be a way."

Elizabeth nodded. She was thinking about what Jessica had said before. If only Bruce were on their side, maybe they could change his father's mind. It seemed to be their only chance.

But how would they ever talk Bruce into it?

CHAPTER 6

# The Rescue Mission

On Monday afternoon Jessica and Elizabeth met several of their friends at the park. The twins loved going to the park after school because they were allowed to ride their bicycles there by themselves.

"Who wants to play freeze tag?" Jessica asked.

"Not again," Lila replied. "We always play that."

Amy nudged Elizabeth with her elbow. "There's Bruce Patman, showing off his fancy bike. He thinks he's so great."

Bruce was near the jungle gym. He was sitting on a brand-new BMX bicycle.

"Come on," Jessica said. "I'm going to tell him off for littering at our garden."

She marched off with Elizabeth, Lila, and Amy right behind her.

"Here come the gardeners," Bruce said when he saw them approaching. He noticed Elizabeth examining his bicycle. "Pretty cool, huh? But this isn't a girl's bike."

"A girl could ride it if she wanted to," Jessica said hotly.

Bruce ignored her. "I have a three-wheel motorbike, too," he boasted to the others. "For off-road riding."

"Oh, who cares?" Elizabeth said. "A motorbike only makes more pollution."

"Pollution?" Bruce laughed. "Who cares about that?"

Jessica frowned. "Just because your father is rich doesn't mean you can do whatever you want. You can't buy more clean air once it's all gone. Ecology is important to everyone."

"Hey!" Eva shouted from the other side of the playground. "Come here, quick!"

Everyone turned to see what was wrong. Eva was kneeling on the ground near some bushes. Jessica, Elizabeth, and their friends ran over. Bruce followed them. "She probably found a gum wrapper on the ground and wants you expert garbage collectors to come over and pick it up," he said, laughing loudly at his own joke.

"What is it?" Elizabeth asked Eva worriedly when she reached her side.

"It's a sea gull," Eva explained. "And it's hurt!"

Elizabeth and the others saw that the injured sea gull was lying on the ground beneath a bush. A plastic six-pack holder was tangled around its neck and left wing. Every time it struggled to get free, it only tangled itself more. There was no way it would be able to get back to the nearby Pacific Ocean if it couldn't fly.

"It can hardly even move!" Jessica cried. "Is its wing broken?"

The sea gull watched them with its round,

frightened eyes. It tried again to free itself but could only flop a short distance.

"We have to help it," Eva said. She sounded as though she were about to cry.

Bruce peered over their shoulders to see what was going on. "What is it?" he asked in a bored voice.

"That's what pollution does!" Jessica shouted as she whirled around to face him. She felt so angry at his careless attitude that she wanted to scream. "Somebody like you littered, and now this poor bird can't even fly!"

Bruce stared down at the sea gull. For once, he didn't respond with a wisecrack or a boast. He just gulped.

"We have to save it," Elizabeth said, gently reaching one hand toward the bird. It squawked faintly and tried to get away.

"Well, so what's the big deal?" Bruce finally said in a loud voice. "The park manager is right over there. He can fix this dumb old bird."

Eva sprang up and ran to get the park manager. The others stood silently, watching the sea gull.

When the park manager arrived, he carefully picked up the sea gull and held it so that it couldn't struggle. "Thanks for telling me about this," he said, softly stroking the frightened bird's head. "If only people would throw their trash in garbage cans instead of on the ground, things like this wouldn't happen."

Jessica nodded. "Will the bird be OK?" she wanted to know.

The park manager took a pair of scissors out of his pants pocket. "Once I cut the plastic off, it'll be just fine," he reassured them. "I don't think its wing is broken."

Sure enough, as soon as it was free of the plastic, the sea gull flew away. It had not been harmed—this time, at least.

Bruce watched the bird take off and then ran back to his bicycle. He jumped on and pedaled away without looking back.

## CHAPTER 7

# On the TV News

"Are there any questions so far about ecology?" Mrs. Otis asked at the beginning of science class the next day.

Elizabeth raised her hand. "Eva found a sea gull yesterday that was caught in a plastic six-pack ring."

Everyone who had been there began talking all at once. Mrs. Otis listened, looking very serious.

"Unfortunately, much of our garbage has been dumped in the ocean for many years," she said. "Things like paper and food dissolve in water. But plastic lasts for years and years."

Elizabeth raised her hand again. "Do a lot of birds get stuck like that?"

Mrs. Otis nodded. "Yes. Birds, otters, dolphins, fish, seals—"

"Seals?" Jessica broke in. Seals were one of her favorite animals.

"Yes," the teacher replied. "All sorts of animals die every year from getting trapped in old plastic nets that are left in the water or from eating plastic they mistake for food. Some animals get plastic rings caught around their necks, and choke to death. As you know, otters are very curious little animals, and they like to play with the things they find. They don't know that plastic can kill them."

Elizabeth felt like crying. She couldn't stand thinking of all the animals who were being hurt that way.

"That's why we have to be extra careful about our environment," Mrs. Otis said, looking at the class solemnly. "The trash we make today might still be around in fifty or a hundred years, hurting animals and polluting the water and the air."

"Mrs. Otis?" Todd spoke up. "My mother always cuts our six-pack rings into little pieces with scissors so that no animal can get caught in them. She learned that from Dr. Snapturtle."

Dr. Snapturtle was a veterinarian who had a weekly television show called *Dr. Snapturtle's Animal Hour*. It was one of the twins' favorite programs. They loved learning about the many wonderful animals that Dr. Snapturtle had on the show.

"Dr. Snapturtle always gives excellent advice," Mrs. Otis said with a smile. "If you have to buy things that use those plastic rings at all, that's a good way to make them safer."

Everyone in class was quiet, and Elizabeth was sure they were all thinking about the things Mrs. Otis had said just as she was. She promised herself that she would start cutting up six-pack rings before throwing them away.

"Speaking of Dr. Snapturtle." Mrs. Otis went on. "It just so happens that we will be going to a taping of the show in two weeks. It's our next class trip."

"Hurray!" everyone shouted.

Jessica was as excited as her classmates, but she couldn't stop thinking about Bruce Patman and his father.

"Psst," she whispered, passing a note to Elizabeth.

Elizabeth opened it and read, "*We have to keep our garden a garden.*"

She looked at Jessica and nodded.

Late that afternoon, Mrs. Wakefield announced that they were going to pick up Mr. Wakefield at his office. As they drove downtown, Elizabeth spoke up.

"Mom, can we stop at the garden again?" she asked.

"I suppose so," their mother said. She turned onto Maple Street.

"There's that TV news van again!" Jessica said, pointing.

They all got out of the car. Mike and some of the other volunteers from Keep Sweet Valley Sweet were doing some chores in the garden. A news crew was filming them.

"Hi, girls," Mike said when he saw Elizabeth and Jessica.

"Are these some of your student helpers?" the camera man asked.

"They certainly are," said Mike. "They're two of my very best workers."

"We worked all day Saturday to make this garden," Jessica explained.

"How about telling us about it on camera?" the man asked. "Both of you. We don't get many identical twin gardeners on the news."

Elizabeth felt a little bit nervous but excited, too. Being on the news would be fun, and it would give them a chance to explain how important the garden was.

"Can you tell us why you volunteered to work on this project?" the man asked, pointing the camera at them.

Jessica stood up very straight and cleared her throat. She had always wanted to be interviewed on television. "We think gardens are more important than parking garages," she explained. "Because—"

Elizabeth looked up to see why Jessica had stopped speaking. Then her heart skipped a beat. Bruce Patman and his father had just arrived.

## CHAPTER 8

# A Special Invitation

Jessica glared at Bruce. She was sure he was only there to cause more trouble. She was afraid that he was going to say that Mr. Patman had won and they had lost despite all their hard work.

"You get out of here," Jessica said, running over to Bruce. "We don't want to listen to you anymore. You don't care about ecology or our environment or anything. You're just a big jerk."

For once, Bruce didn't start bragging. Instead he shook his head. "I have something to tell you," he said in a quiet voice. He looked a little bit embarrassed as he glanced at his father. Mr. Patman was talking in a loud, confident voice to the TV news crew.

Bruce cleared his throat. "I wanted to tell you that I'm on your side."

Jessica's mouth dropped open in surprise. "What?"

"I think I know how I can get my dad to give up the whole plan about the garage," Bruce went on.

Elizabeth and Jessica stared at one another. "What made you change your mind?" Jessica asked.

"I don't know," Bruce said with a shrug. He looked at the ground and kicked a pebble.

"I know," Elizabeth said suddenly. "It was the sea gull, right?"

"So what if it was?" Bruce asked.

He sounded like his old, stuck-up self again. But that didn't matter to Jessica. He was on their side now.

"OK, what's the plan?" she asked.

"My dad likes people to think he's a good guy," Bruce explained. "He goes to a lot of fancy dinners for good causes and charities and things. So maybe if you invited him for a picnic here, and a lot of people showed up, he'd change his mind because he'd see that it would make so many people happy."

Jessica looked around at all the trees and flowers. "Do you really think it'll work?" she asked.

"It might," Bruce said. "But you have to do it soon."

"We will," Elizabeth said, nodding. "It's our only chance."

At school the next day, Jessica and Elizabeth told Mrs. Otis and their whole class about Bruce's suggestion.

"I think it could work," Lila said. "My father goes to parties all the time where they ask for donations and things."

"Well, we can't expect miracles," Mrs. Otis said seriously. "You have to understand that there's a lot of money at stake, and that no matter how much we want to, we may not be able to change Mr. Patman's mind."

Jessica looked at the floor. It sounded as if Mrs. Otis didn't think Bruce's plan would work.

Then the teacher's face broke into a smile. "But I think it's worth a try. We should do everything we can to save our garden and to stand up for the environment. Do we all agree?" she asked. "Should we try Bruce Patman's idea? Let's see a show of hands."

Every student in the class raised his or her hand to vote for the plan. Jessica looked at Elizabeth and smiled. "Cross your fingers."

Caroline Pearce raised her hand. "Let's make a fancy invitation," she suggested.

"We could use our recycled paper," Jessica suggested.

"Excellent idea," Mrs. Otis said.

The papers the class had torn up last week had been cooked in water on a hot plate Mrs. Otis brought in. Then the paper shreds had been soaked in a special chemical before being pressed on a screen and left to dry. The recycled paper was a little bit gray and bumpy, but it could be used for many things.

"Let's decide what to put on the invitation," Mrs. Otis said.

While Eva, Amy, and Todd picked out the best sheet of recycled paper, the others made suggestions.

"We could draw the garden on it," Elizabeth said.

"I know!" Jessica raised her hand. "Let's draw the Earth. Because the whole Earth should be like a garden. And Mrs. Otis said the garden is our way of making the whole world a little bit greener."

Mrs. Otis smiled at Jessica. "Who wants to do that?" she asked the class.

Almost everyone voted for Jessica's idea. Sandy Ferris was the best artist in the class, so she was elected to draw the Earth.

"Sandy, make sure you draw a flower growing out of the earth," Ellen said. "To show where our garden is."

Jessica was so excited about their invitation that she could hardly sit still. She was sure that Mr. Patman would see how important it was to keep the garden. Sandy began drawing a globe, and Eva offered to write the invitation.

"I'd like each of you to sign the card after Eva has written the message," Mrs. Otis said. "We all worked on the garden, and the invitation should be from all of us."

Soon the card was finished. Jessica thought it was perfect. All they had to do now was deliver it to Bruce.

## CHAPTER 9

# A Wet Picnic

Saturday was the day of the picnic. The moment Elizabeth woke up, she ran to the window to see what the weather was like. Almost every day in southern California was sunny.

Except for this one.

"I hope it doesn't rain," she said as she began to get dressed.

"Me, too. Mr. Patman has to see it our way," Jessica said nervously. "He just has to."

After breakfast, Elizabeth and Jessica helped their mother make a lentil salad. They chopped up carrots and parsley and tomatoes while Mrs. Wakefield made the dressing.

"Everyone is bringing natural food," Elizabeth told her mother. "And we're going to use paper cups and plates."

"It's going to be a totally natural picnic," Jessica explained proudly. "Except for the plastic forks. But we won't leave any on the ground. We're going to bring them home and wash them so we can use them again. Mrs. Otis says that's another small thing we can do that will make a big difference to the environment."

Mrs. Wakefield spooned their salad into a large plastic container. "You girls certainly know your stuff. I don't know how Mr. Patman could possibly resist your arguments," she said, giving each of them a kiss. "Good luck."

Eva's mother picked them up. Elizabeth, Jessica, and Eva sat in the backseat, looking out the windows at the gloomy, gray sky. "Rain, rain, go away, come again another day," Jessica chanted.

"Mr. Patman is definitely coming, isn't he?" Eva asked.

"Bruce said he would," Elizabeth said. "I hope he's right."

"Here we are," Mrs. Simpson said. "Good luck, girls."

Elizabeth, Jessica, and Eva got out of the car with their food. Many of their classmates were already at the garden, spreading blankets on the ground and arranging stacks of paper plates and cups.

"Is he here yet?" Jessica asked, looking around.

Lila shook her head. "Not yet."

Nobody was talking much. Everyone was too worried.

"Here he comes!" Todd shouted.

They all watched in silence as Mr. Patman and Bruce stepped out of their limousine. Mr. Patman walked toward the group with a wide, jovial smile.

"Well, well," he said in a hearty voice. "I

haven't been invited to a picnic in a long time. Isn't this a pretty spot?"

Elizabeth could tell he didn't really mean it. He smiled, but she was sure he was just being polite. She just hoped that they could change his mind.

"The kids would like to give you a tour of the garden, Mr. Patman," Mrs. Otis said. "They've put in a lot of hard work here, and they're very proud of what they've done."

In single file, they led Mr. Patman up and down the wood-chip pathways. Elizabeth was too nervous to say anything, and so was everyone else. Mrs. Otis pointed out the handmade benches, the birdbath, the trees, and every part of the project that the students helped with. Mr. Patman smiled and nodded politely.

"Now, how about starting our picnic?" Mrs. Otis suggested.

Elizabeth looked up at the sky. It was getting darker by the minute.

"Rain, rain, go away," Jessica whispered under her breath.

As everyone filled their plates with food, there was a loud clap of thunder.

"Oh no!" Lila screamed, covering her head.

Rain began pouring out of the sky. Elizabeth tried to pick up a blanket, while Mrs. Otis grabbed a platter full of cold fried chicken. Everybody tried to cover the food and stay dry at the same time. Some of the kids ran under the little trees for shelter. The birdbath quickly filled to the top and overflowed.

"Oh, no," Elizabeth moaned, hiding under a blanket with Jessica. "Everything is ruined. Now he'll never change his mind!"

The only person who wasn't trying to get out of the rain was Mr. Patman. He was sitting on a bench with water dripping down his face—and he was laughing.

"I haven't been caught in the rain in a long

time!" he said, chuckling. "But if you have to get drenched, this is a nice place for it."

Elizabeth and Jessica stared at him. He looked like he was having fun!

Then, as quickly as the rain had started, it stopped. The clouds parted, and sunlight came streaming down. One by one, the kids came out from their hiding places and looked around. Raindrops sparkled brilliantly on every leaf and twig.

"This is beautiful," Mr. Patman said in a loud voice. "Look at those flowers! Look how green the grass is!"

"Do you really like it, Dad?" Bruce asked his father timidly.

Mr. Patman didn't answer. "Tell me, son," he said in a stern voice. "What made *you* so serious about this garden?"

Bruce gulped. He looked a little bit nervous, as though he wasn't used to standing up to his father. "I just think it's a good idea to keep it this way, so birds and squirrels and other animals will have a nice place to live."

"Hmmm . . ." Mr. Patman said with a frown.

"Can we keep the garden the way it is?" Jessica asked. "Please?"

Mr. Patman was silent for a moment while he wiped some water from his forehead. Just when Jessica thought she couldn't stand the suspense for another moment, Mr. Patman cleared his throat and looked around at them all. "I've made my decision," he announced. "I'm definitely going to buy this piece of land."

Elizabeth and Jessica looked at one another, too disappointed to speak. They had lost.

## CHAPTER 10

# Victory

"But Dad!" Bruce gasped.

Tears came to Jessica's eyes. Her plan had failed. They had worked so hard to clean up the pollution in one little spot, and all their effort had been for nothing.

"I'm going to buy this piece of land," Mr. Patman repeated. "And I'm going to keep it exactly the way it is. Who could be heartless enough to cover a lovely spot like this with a parking garage?"

Jessica threw her paper cup in the air, sending juice splashing everywhere. "Hurray!" she yelled. Then she picked up her cup again.

"Mr. Patman, we are so thankful for your decision," Mrs. Otis said with a delighted smile. "I'm sure you won't regret it."

"I'm sure I won't," Mr. Patman agreed. "Right now, I think the most important thing is to finish our picnic. That shower gave me a huge appetite."

Jessica felt so relieved that she sat down on the wet grass. It made her happy to think that from now on, there would always be a little green island in the middle of their city.

And it was all thanks to them. And Bruce. And Mr. Patman.

She looked over at Bruce and smiled. Maybe he wasn't so bad, after all.

"Hurry up!" Elizabeth said when they got home from school the following Monday. "It's almost time for *Dr. Snapturtle's Animal Hour.*"

Jessica followed her sister into the den and turned on the television.

"Won't it be fun to see him in person?"

Jessica asked as she sat down on the couch. "We've never been to a live TV show taping before. I'm definitely going to raise my hand when he asks for volunteers."

Elizabeth smiled. "Dr. Snapturtle is the best. And so is Duke," she said. Duke was the veterinarian's dog who was on the show every day.

Jessica and Elizabeth hummed along with the theme music. Dr. Snapturtle was their hero. They couldn't wait to meet him and get his autograph.

***What will Dr. Snapturtle be like in person? Find out in Sweet Valley Kids #28,* ELIZABETH MEETS HER HERO.**